Originally published as *Luuk en Lotje. Het is Pasen!* in Belgium and the Netherlands by Clavis Uitgeverij, 2019
English translation from the Dutch by Clavis Publishing Inc., New York

Visit us on the Web at www.clavis-publishing.com.

Luke and Lottie. It's Easter! written and illustrated by Ruth Wielockx

ISBN 978-1-60537-525-0 (hardcover edition)
ISBN 978-1-60537-526-7 (softcover edition)

This book was printed in October 2019 at Nikara, M. R. Štefánika 858/25, 963 01 Krupina, Slovakia.

First Edition
10 9 8 7 6 5 4 3 2 1

Luke and Lottie

It's Easter!

Clavis

NEW YORK

It's Easter!
Luke and Lottie are going to the farm
for an Easter egg hunt.

"I hope I find fifty eggs," says Lottie.
"I want to find one hundred!" says Luke.

Hey, who's sitting at the breakfast table? Is it the Easter Bunny?
No, it's Daddy! He looks funny in his bunny costume.
"We want to put on our bunny suits too!" say Luke and Lottie.
"After you eat your breakfast," says Mommy.

Luke and Lottie put on their bunny suits.
They hop around their room.
"Let's go, sweet bunnies! We don't want to be late
for the Easter egg hunt," Mommy says with a laugh.
Hop, hop, hop!

Luke and Lottie get a ride to the farm.
"I can't see a thing," Luke calls. "My ears are covering my eyes!"
"There!" Lottie points. "I can see the farm."

"Happy Easter! And welcome to my farm," says Farmer Fred.
"I see lots of great costumes here!"
Luke and Lottie see a rabbit, a sheep, a chick ...
There's even a girl dressed up as an Easter egg!

It's time for the egg hunt to begin.
The children grab their baskets,
and Farmer Fred rings the bell.
Ring ring!

Luke and Lottie run to the henhouse first.
"Look!" says Luke. "A brown chicken. Maybe she lays chocolate eggs!"
Oh no! It's definitely not a chocolate egg . . .
"I found a chocolate egg!" Lottie calls. "Look—there is another one!"

Luke and Lottie gather more colored eggs and put them in their baskets. The lambs in the meadow follow along.

Now Luke and Lottie run to the bunny hutch.
"Wow, so many Easter Bunnies!" calls Luke.
"Those are real bunnies," laughs Lottie.
They collect more and more eggs.
"My basket is full, " says Luke.

It's time to go home. Mommy is bringing some fresh eggs home, and Daddy has some branches.
"What are we going to do with those branches?" asks Lottie.

"You'll see when we get home," says Mommy.
"Okay! Bye, Farmer Fred!"
Luke and Lottie call as they wave goodbye.

At home Luke and Lottie use paint and colored feathers
to decorate some eggs of their own.
Lottie paints her egg very carefully.
Luke likes to use the feathers. Some go on the eggs.
Some go in the air! Wheee!

Mommy helps them put ribbons on the eggs.
Then Luke and Lottie hang the eggs on the branches.
What a beautiful Easter egg tree!
Happy Easter!

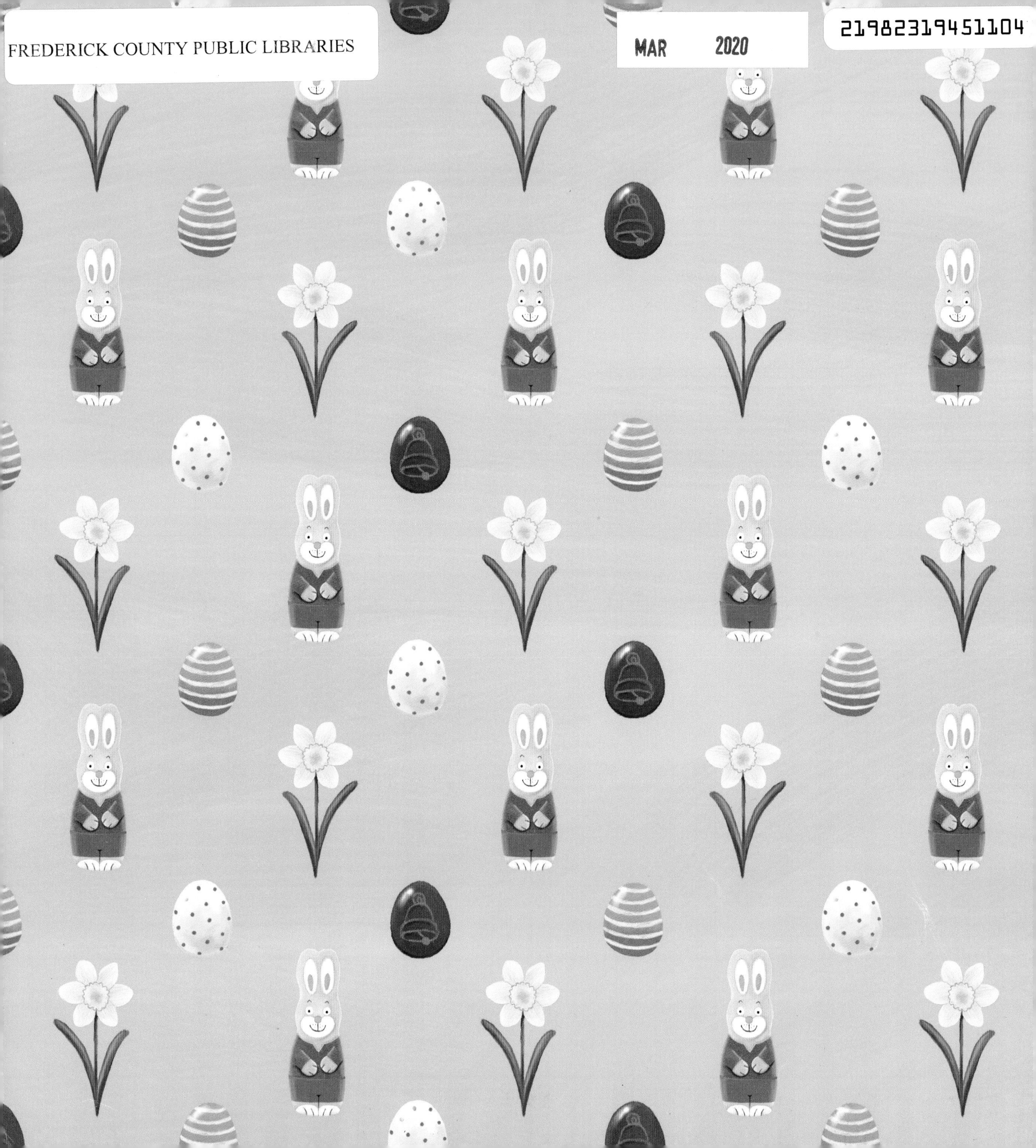